Owliver

by Robert Kraus

pictures by

Jose Aruego & Ariane Dewey

Prentice-Hall Books for Young Readers
A Division of Simon & Schuster, Inc.
New York

Published by Prentice-Hall Books for Young Readers,
A Division of Simon & Schuster, Inc.
Simon & Schuster Building
Rockefeller Center
1230 Avenue of the Americas
New York, NY 10020

Originally published by Windmill Books, Inc.
and Wanderer Books, a division of Simon & Schuster, Inc.

Prentice-Hall Books for Young Readers
is a trademark of Simon & Schuster, Inc.

Manufactured in the United States of America

10 9 8 7 6 5 4 3 2 1

Library of Congress Cataloging in Publication Data

Kraus, Robert, 1925
  Owliver.

  SUMMARY: Although each of his parents expects him
to be different things when he grows up, a little owl
decides for himself what to be.
  [1. Individuality—Fiction.   2. Owls—Fiction]
1. Aruego, Jose.   II.   Dewey, Ariane.   III.   Title.
PZ7.K868Ow   1980   [E]   80-13664
ISBN 0-13-647538-8

For Augusta Baker,
who likes Owls

"I am an orphan."

"I have no father."

"I have no mother."

"I don't have anybody,"
said Owliver.

"Don't be silly," said Owliver's father.
"You do have a father."

"And a mother, too," said Owliver's mother.

"I know," said Owliver.
"I was just acting. I like to act."

Owliver acted all day.

Owliver acted all night.

"Owliver is so talented,"
said Owliver's mother.
"Better he should be a lawyer or a doctor,"
said Owliver's father.

Owliver's father gave him doctor toys

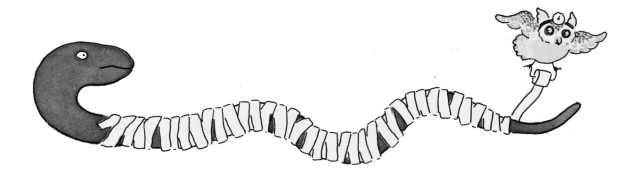

...and lawyer toys.

Owliver's mother gave him acting lessons,

Joy

Anger

Fear

Sadness

Goodness

Hate

Love

...including tap dancing.
"Talent should be encouraged," she said.

Owliver acted out a play
about a doctor and a lawyer who never meet
(because Owliver played both parts).

And he pleased his mother
and he pleased his father.

"Owliver will become a doctor or a lawyer when he grows up," said Owliver's father.

"Owliver will become an actor or a playwright when he grows up," said Owliver's mother.

But
when
Owliver
grew
up,
guess what
he
became...

A FIREMAN!